DRIVING DADDY

by Hope Vestergaard

illustrations by
Thierry Courtin

Dutton Children's Books
New York

Text copyright © 2003 by Hope Vestergaard
Illustrations copyright © 2003 by Thierry Courtin
All rights reserved.

CIP Data is available.

Published in the United States by Dutton Children's Books,
a division of Penguin Putnam Books for Young Readers
345 Hudson Street, New York, New York 10014
www.penguinputnam.com

Designed by Beth Herzog
Printed in China
First Edition
ISBN 0-525-47032-8
10 9 8 7 6 5 4 3 2 1

For Max—
Drive carefully!

H.V.

Way up high, you're driving Daddy!
Big, broad shoulders—comfy seat.
His hands hold you like a seat belt.
Let's drive Daddy down the street.

You're a giant! Watch those branches. . . .
Apple blossoms fill the air.
Use your hands as windshield wipers,
Brush that mess off Daddy's hair.

Wave to neighbors. Look, a doggy!
BEEP BEEP, doggy, clear the way!
Baby's driving to the playground.
He can't wait to park and play!

Hurry, Daddy! Faster, faster!
Squeeze his neck with all your might.
WHEEE! You're speeding. This road's BUMPY!
Hug Dad's forehead, hang on tight!

VROOM, VROOM! Baby's so excited!
There's the park, right by the lake.
Slow down, Daddy! You will miss it!
Pull Dad's hair to hit the brake.

Dad keeps going. What's he doing?
That way, Daddy! See the swing?
Tug those ears and try to steer him—
Someone stop this crazy thing!

Don't you worry, just a detour!
Daddy's got a secret plan.
Something good's around the corner . . .
Hear that music? Ice-cream man!

PHEW! We made it. Just in time, too!
How about an ice-cream bar?
Baby, you're a super driver.
Daddy, you're his perfect car!